MCA
J

P. I. C

W9-CKL-796

ING
16.99

MCA
J

seven hungry babies

seven hungry

ATHENEUM BOOKS FOR YOUNG READERS NEW YORK LONDON TORONTO SYDNEY

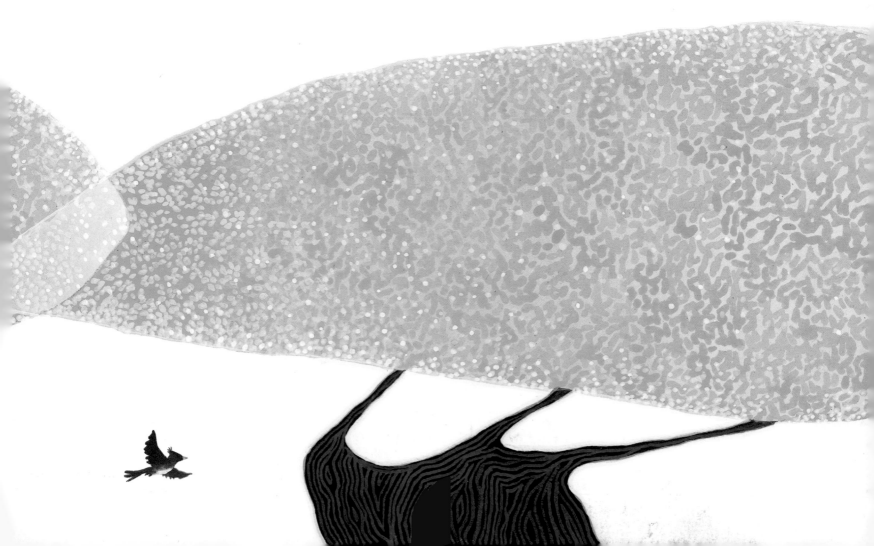

babies

words by candace fleming

pictures by eugene yelchin

One spring morning,
high in a nest,
seven speckled eggs begin to—

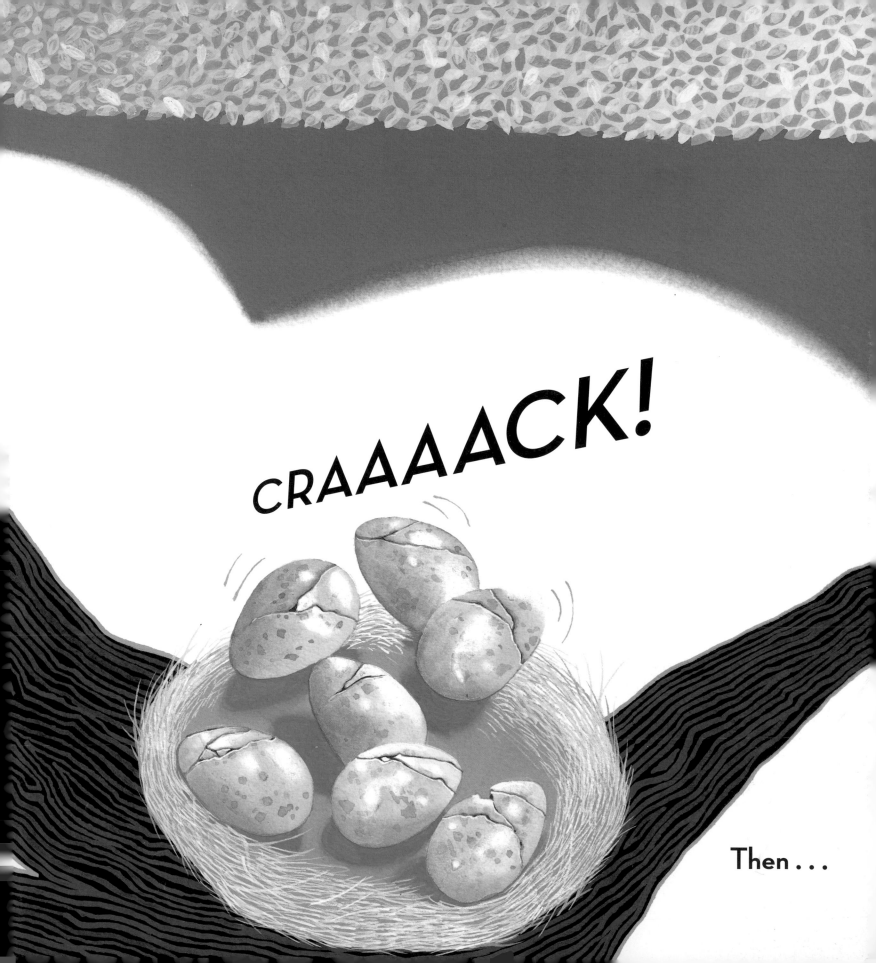

CRAAAACK!

Then . . .

Seven hungry babies open their beaks wide.

"Feed us! Feed us!" the little ones cry.

"Of course, my precious cuddle fluffs," Mama Bird coos.

"I'll fly to the tall grass to find you some food."

Flappa-flap, swoop-swoop, zoom-zoom, yum!

Mama zips back
with a
cricket for one.

G-u-u-u-l-p!

Six hungry babies squirm, stretch, and reach.
"Feed us! Feed us!" the little ones screech.

"Yes, yes,
my noisy warble pies,"
Mama Bird coos.
"I'll fly to the orchard to find you
more food."

Flappa-flap, swoop-swoop, zoom-zoom, **yum!**

Mama flies back

with a

cherry for one.

G-u-u-u-l-p!

Five hungry babies hop up and down.
"Feed us! Feed us!"
The little ones frown.

"Settle down,
sweet hatchlings,"
Mama Bird coos,
"and I'll fly to the school yard
to find you more food."

Flappa-flap, swoop-swoop, pant-pant, **yum!**

Mama puffs back with a bread   crust for one.

G-u-u-u-l-p!

Four hungry babies fret, sulk, and pout.
"Feed us! Feed us!" the little ones shout.

"Hush,
you little egg-crackers,"
Mama Bird coos,
"and I'll fly to the garden
to find you more food."

Flappa-flap, swoop-swoop, pant-pant, **yum!**

Mama limps back
with a
pea pod for one.

G-u-u-u-l-p!

Three hungry babies stamp their tiny feet.
"Feed us! Feed us!" the little ones shriek.

"Give me strength
and patience,"
Mama Bird coos,
"so I can fly to the millpond
to find them more food."

Mama
struggles
back
with a
minnow for
one.

G-u-u-u-l-p!

Two hungry babies thrashing on the floor.
"Feed us! Feed us!" the little ones roar.

"I can do this
for my babies,"
Mama Bird coos.
"I can fly to the feeder to find
them more food."

Flappa-flap, swoop-swoop, drag-drag, **yum!**

Mama
stumbles
back
with
a bird seed
for one.

G-u-u-u-l-p!

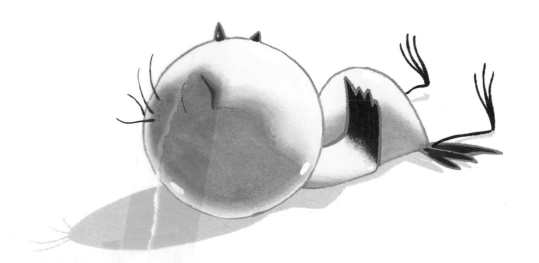

One hungry baby kicks,
nips, and bawls.
"Feed me! Feed me!"
the little one squalls.

But Mama Bird
     can't coo a word.
     She's completely out of breath.
     Wheezing,
     yet determined . . .

she drops down
from the
nest.

Mama staggers back with an earthworm for one.

G-u-u-u-l-p!

Seven quiet babies finally napping in the nest.

"Ah," coos Mama Bird,
"now I get to—"

Peep!

Peep!

Peep!

Seven hungry babies
open their beaks wide.

"Oh, no, not this time," Mama chirps. . . .

"It's Daddy's turn to fly."